DANGER FROM THE DEEP

Written by Dennis "Rocket" Shealy
Illustrated by Loston Wallace

A GOLDEN BOOK • NEW YORK

DC SUPER FRIENDS and all related titles, characters, and elements are trademarks of DC Comics. Copyright © 2009 DC Comics. All rights reserved. Published in the United States by Golden Books, an imprint of Random House Children's Books, a division of Random House, Inc., 1745 Broadway, New York, NY 10019, and in Canada by Random House of Canada Limited, Toronto. Golden Books, A Golden Book, and the G colophon are registered trademarks of Random House, Inc.

ISBN: 978-0-375-85328-9

www.randomhouse.com/kids

Printed in the United States of America

20 19 18 17 16 15 14 13 12

SUPERMAN™

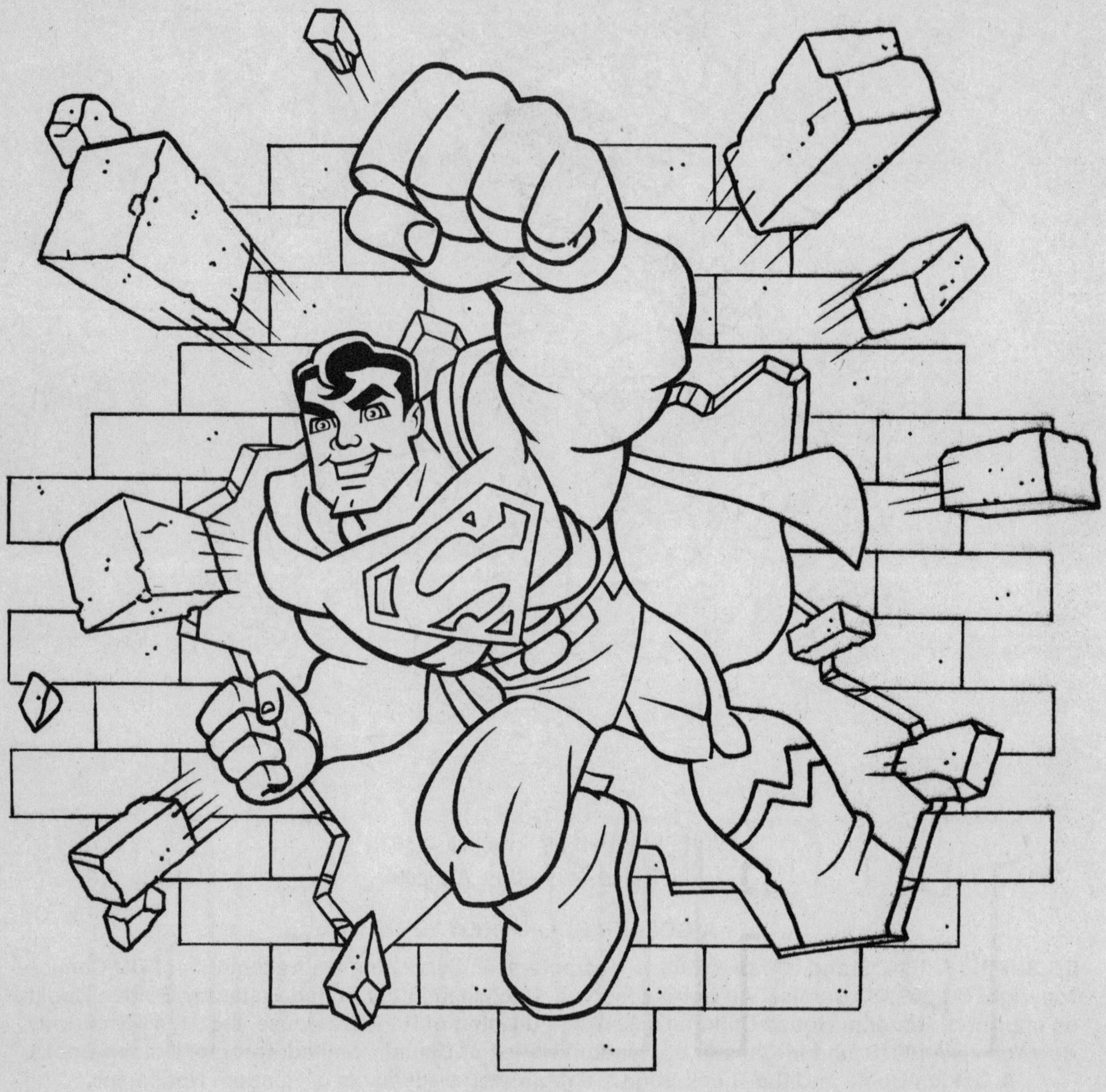

BATMAN™

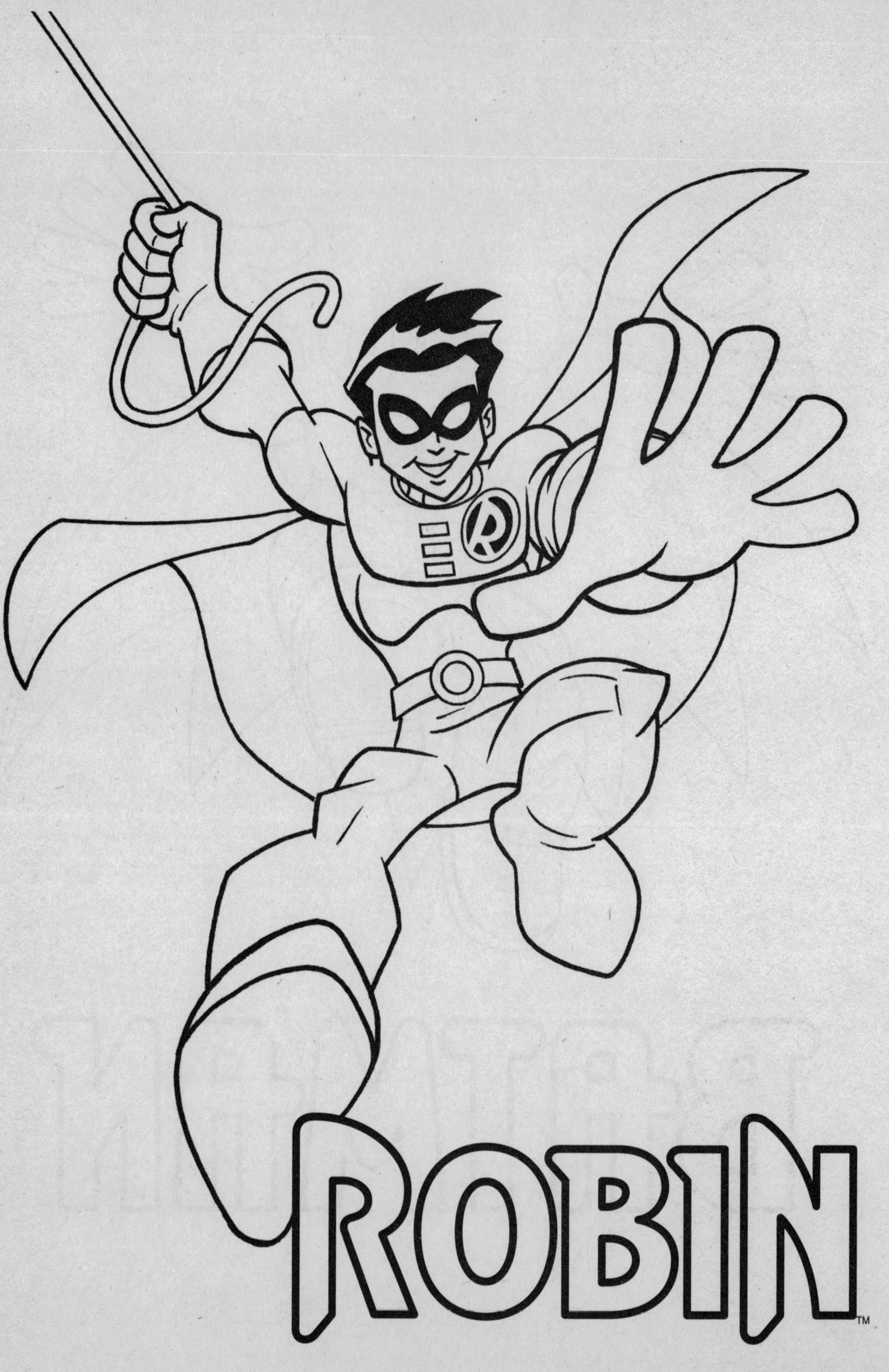
ROBIN™

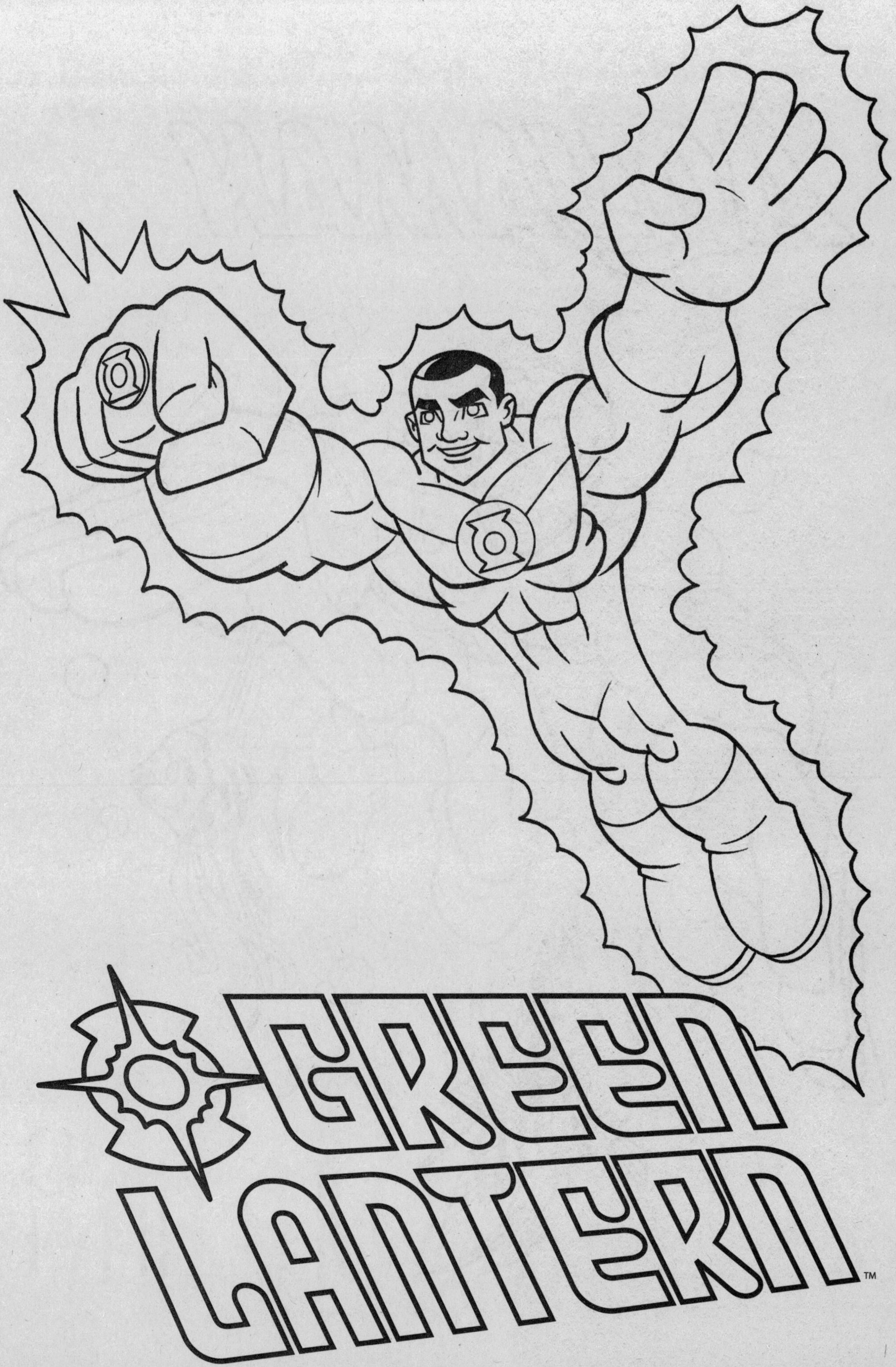
GREEN LANTERN™

AQUAMAN™

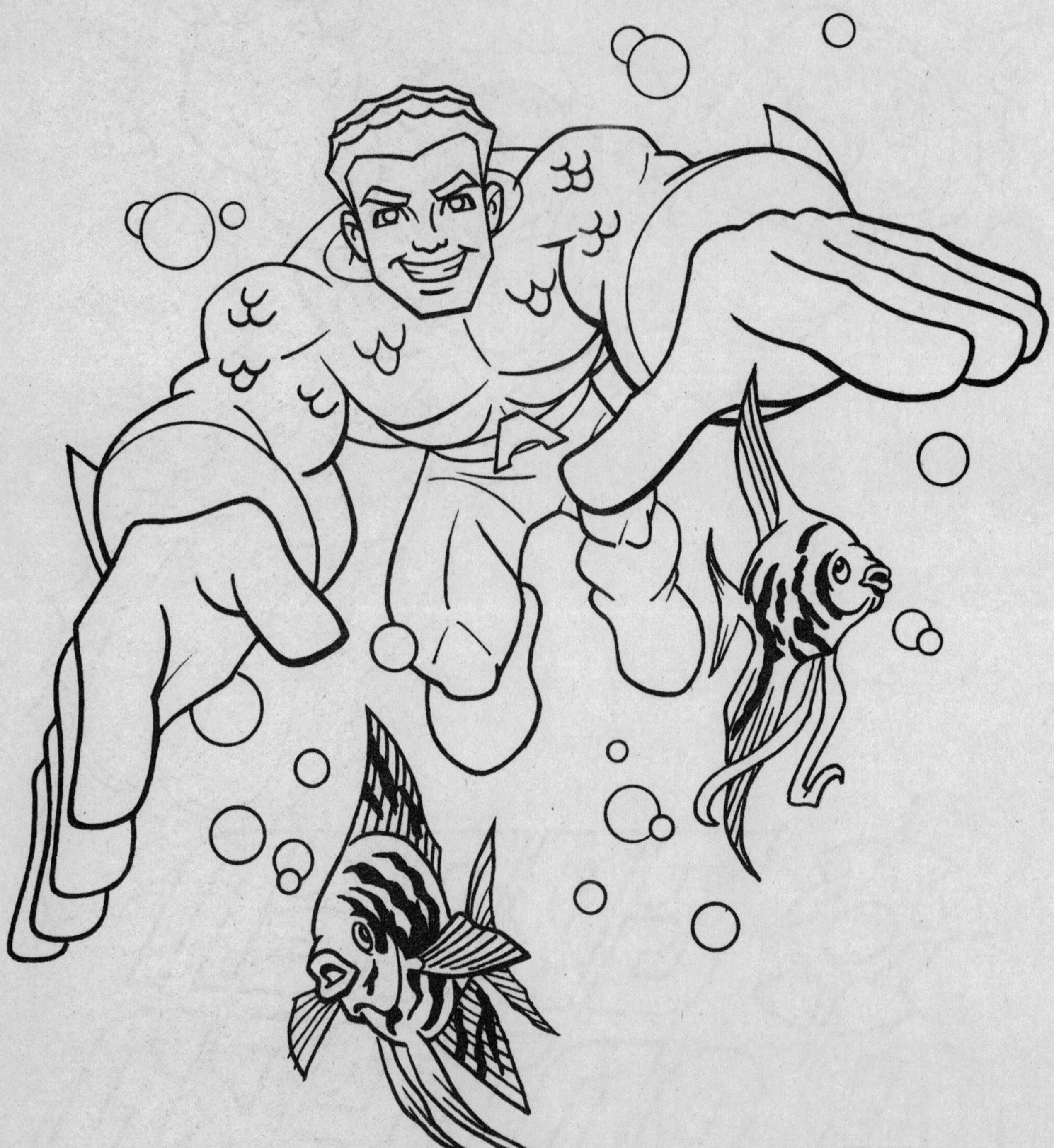

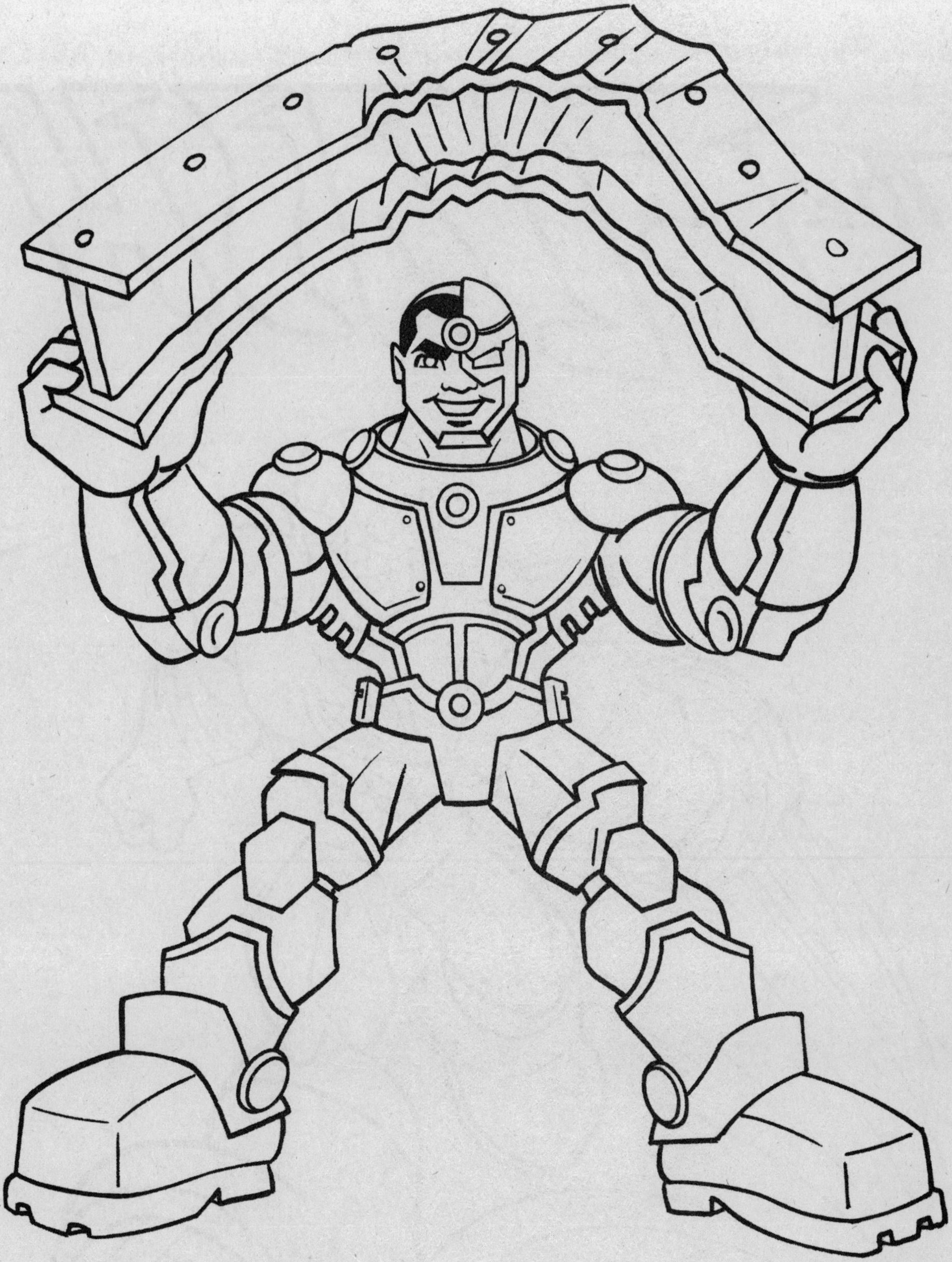

CYBORG™

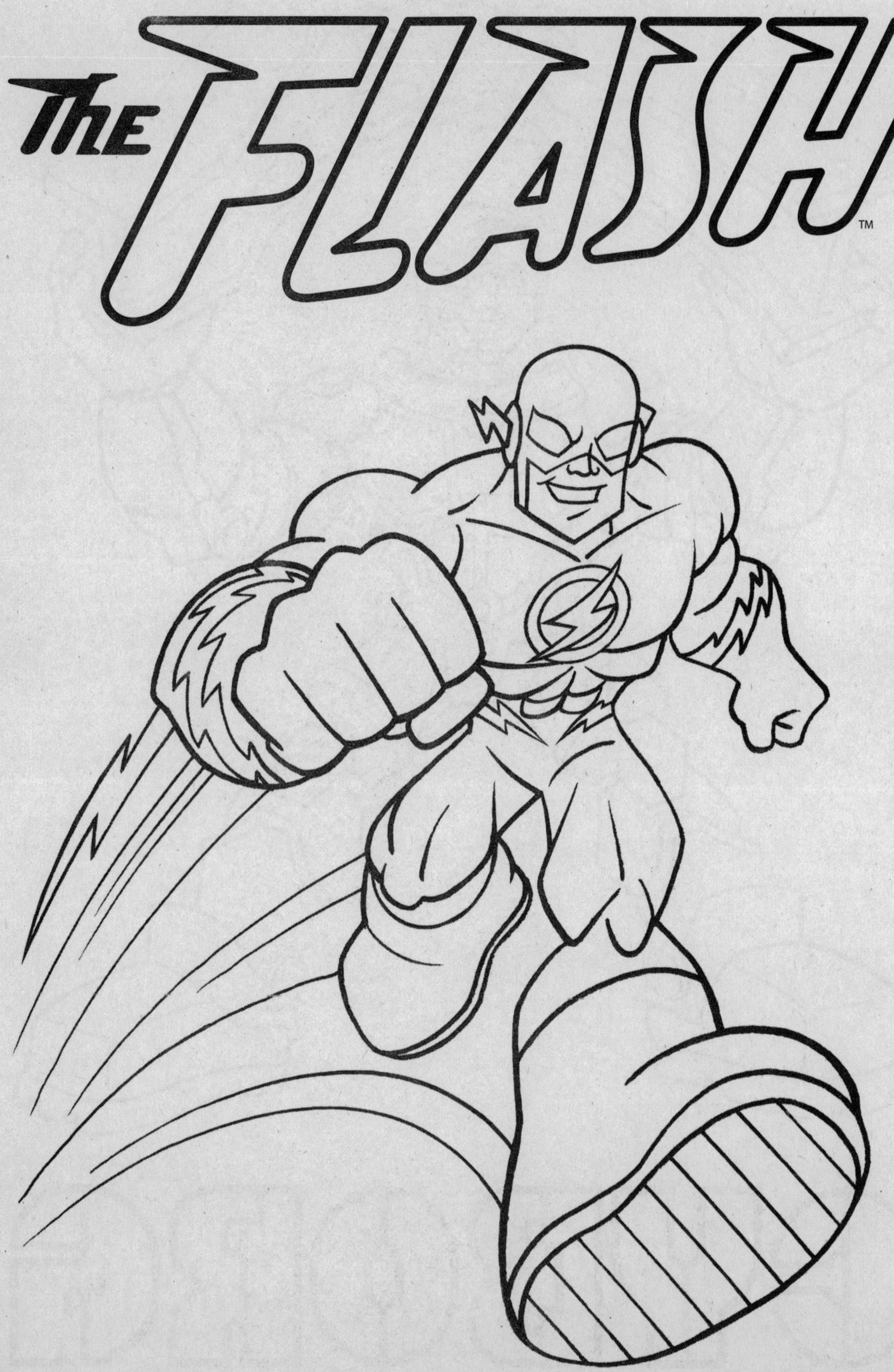

THE FLASH™

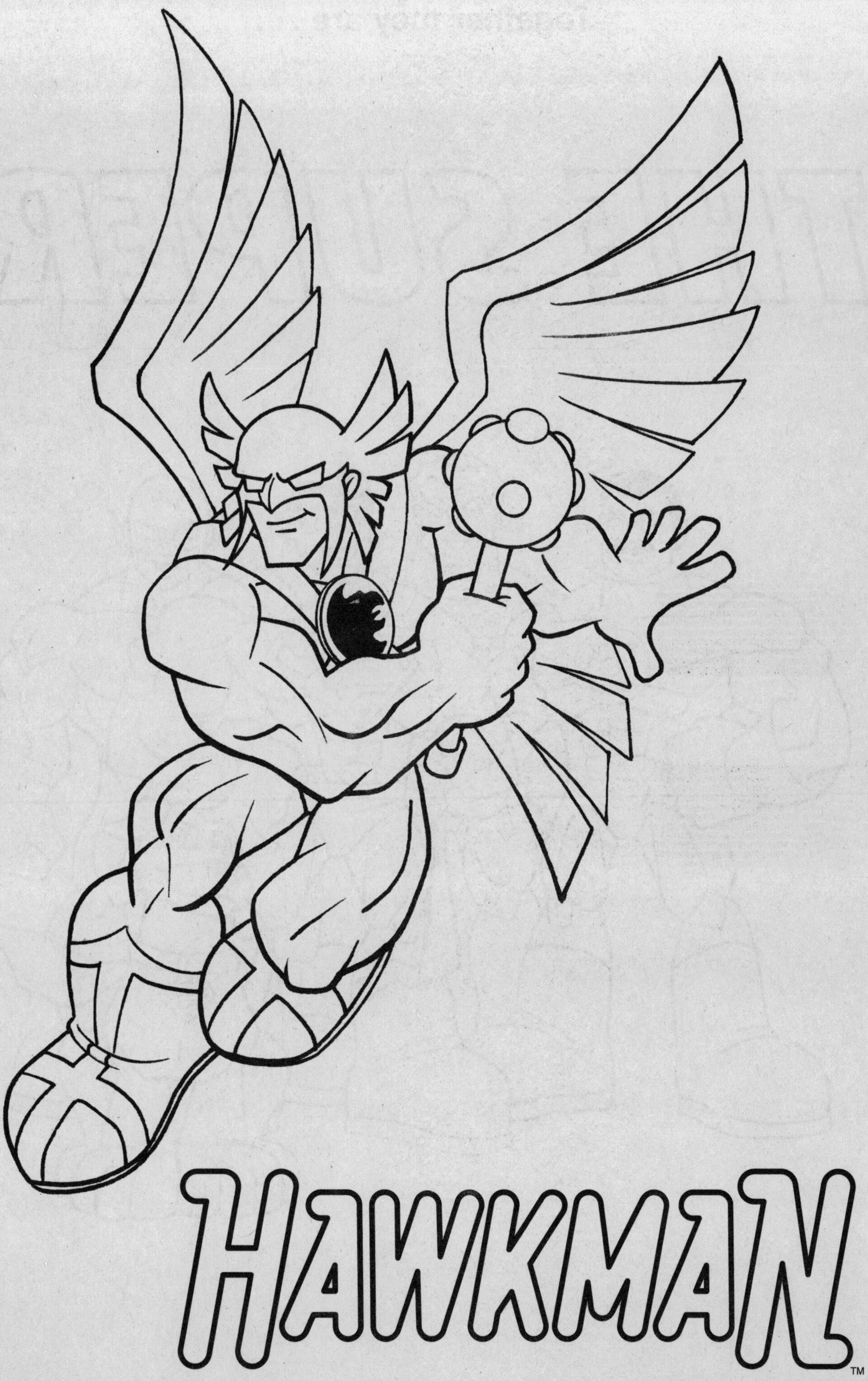

HAWKMAN™

Together they are . . .

THE SUPER

FRIENDS ™

The bad guys are on the loose!

WANTED

LEX LUTHOR

THE PENGUIN

MR. FREEZE

THE JOKER

Lex Luthor is an evil genius.

Watch out for the Penguin's umbrella!

Mr. Freeze is ice-cold.

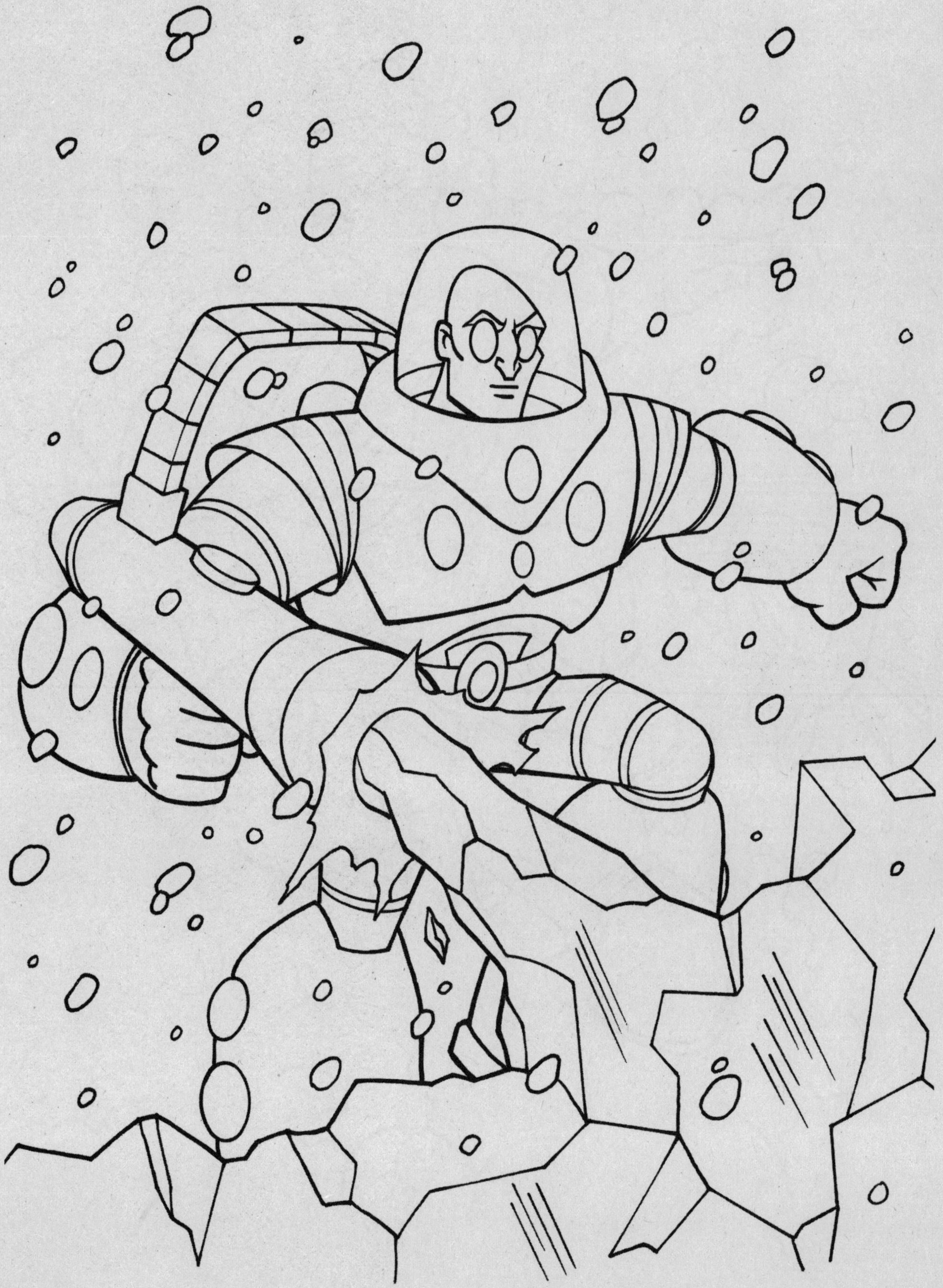

Aquaman senses trouble in the sea.

The fish are frightened.

Something big swims up from deep in the ocean.

A giant octopus!

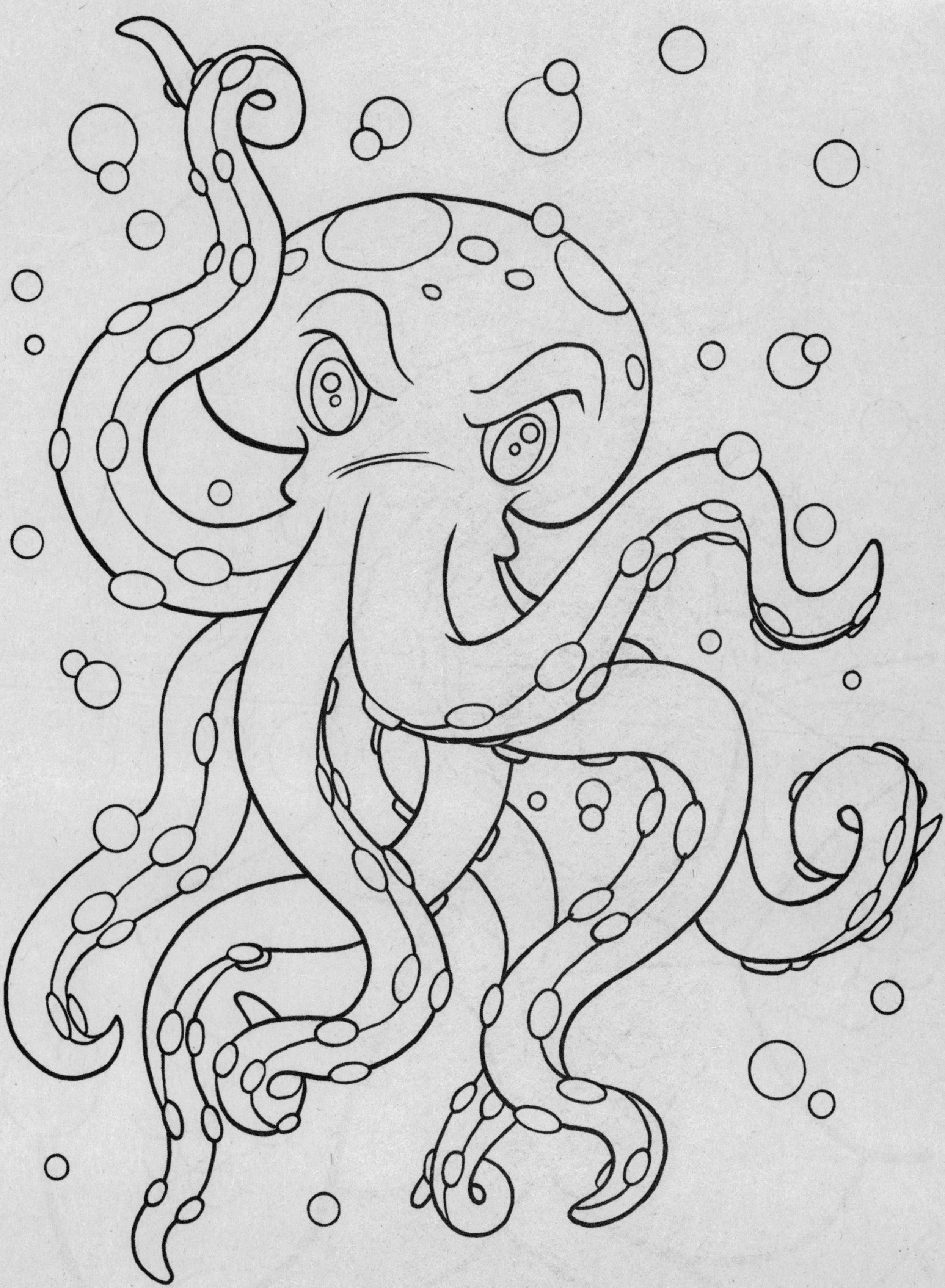

**Aquaman tries to talk to the octopus,
but the beast won't listen.**

"I'd better call the Super Friends," Aquaman says.

The Super Friends are on the way!

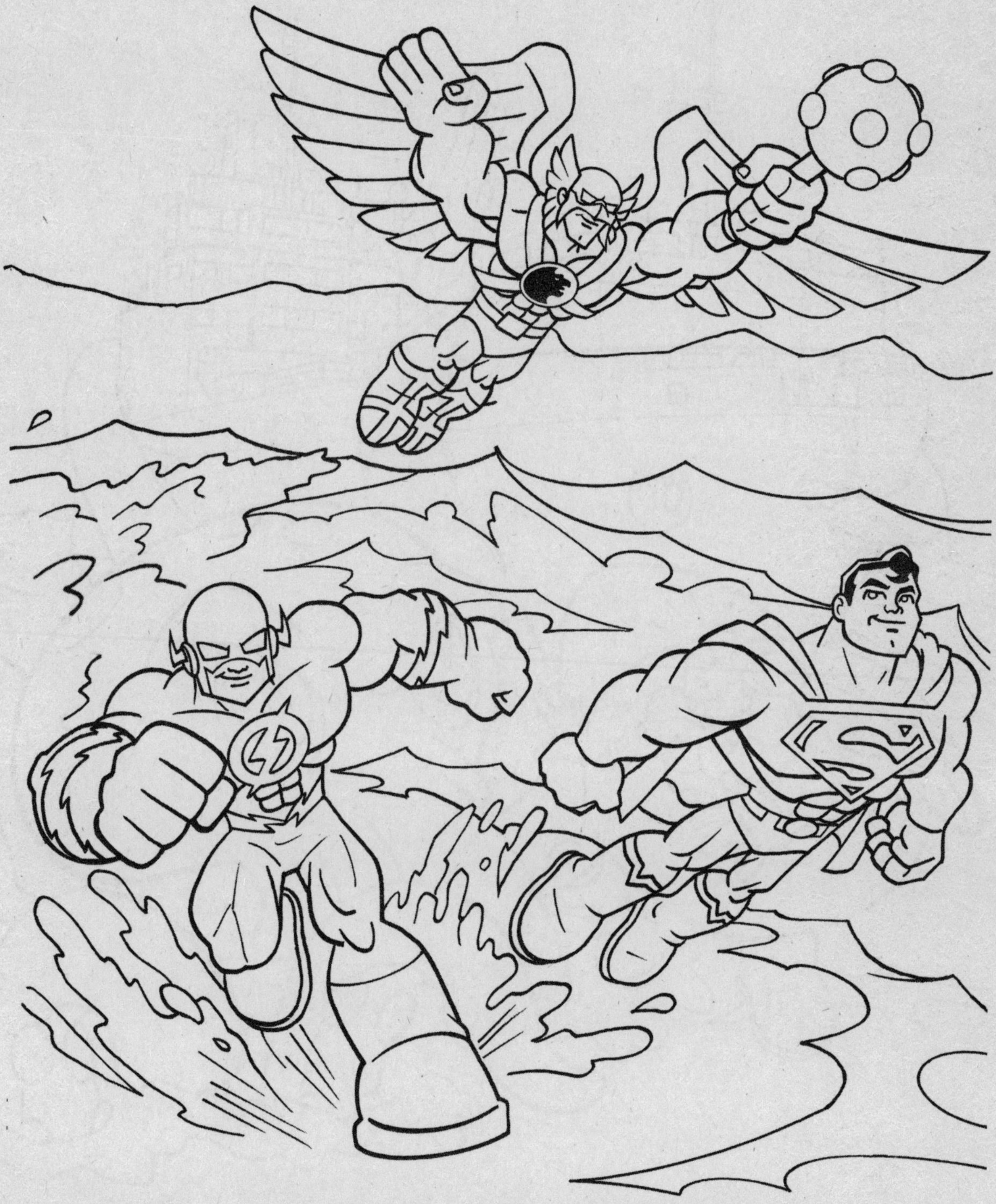

The octopus attacks a ship!

Green Lantern and Hawkman free Aquaman.

"We've got to save the ship," says Batman.

"Leave that to me!" says Cyborg.

Cyborg sends a surge of electricity through the ship.

The octopus gets a shock!

Superman ties up the tentacles.

Batman and Robin snare the sea beast.

**After untying the rope,
the Flash creates a whirlpool.**

The octopus gets sucked beneath the waves!

Great teamwork, Super Friends!

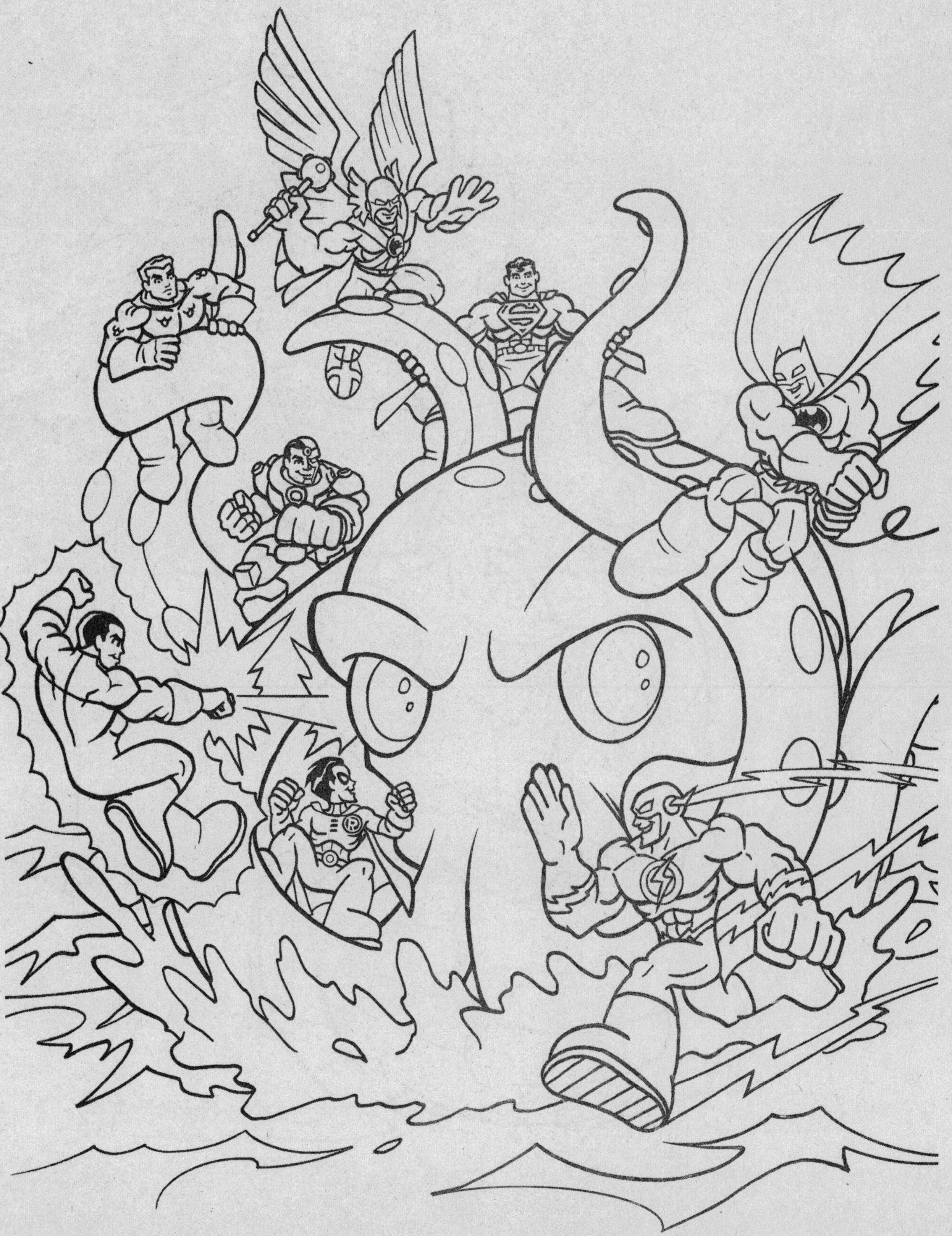

The Joker's toys keep him laughing!

The Flash can run right up walls!

Hawkman stops this bad bird!

Green Lantern protects Earth.

Draw a line to match each Super Friend with his close-up.

Green Lantern lends a hand.

Connect the dots to see Hawkman's favorite weapon.

Batman is also called the Dark Knight.

The Flash is too quick for these bad guys!

Krypto is a superdog!

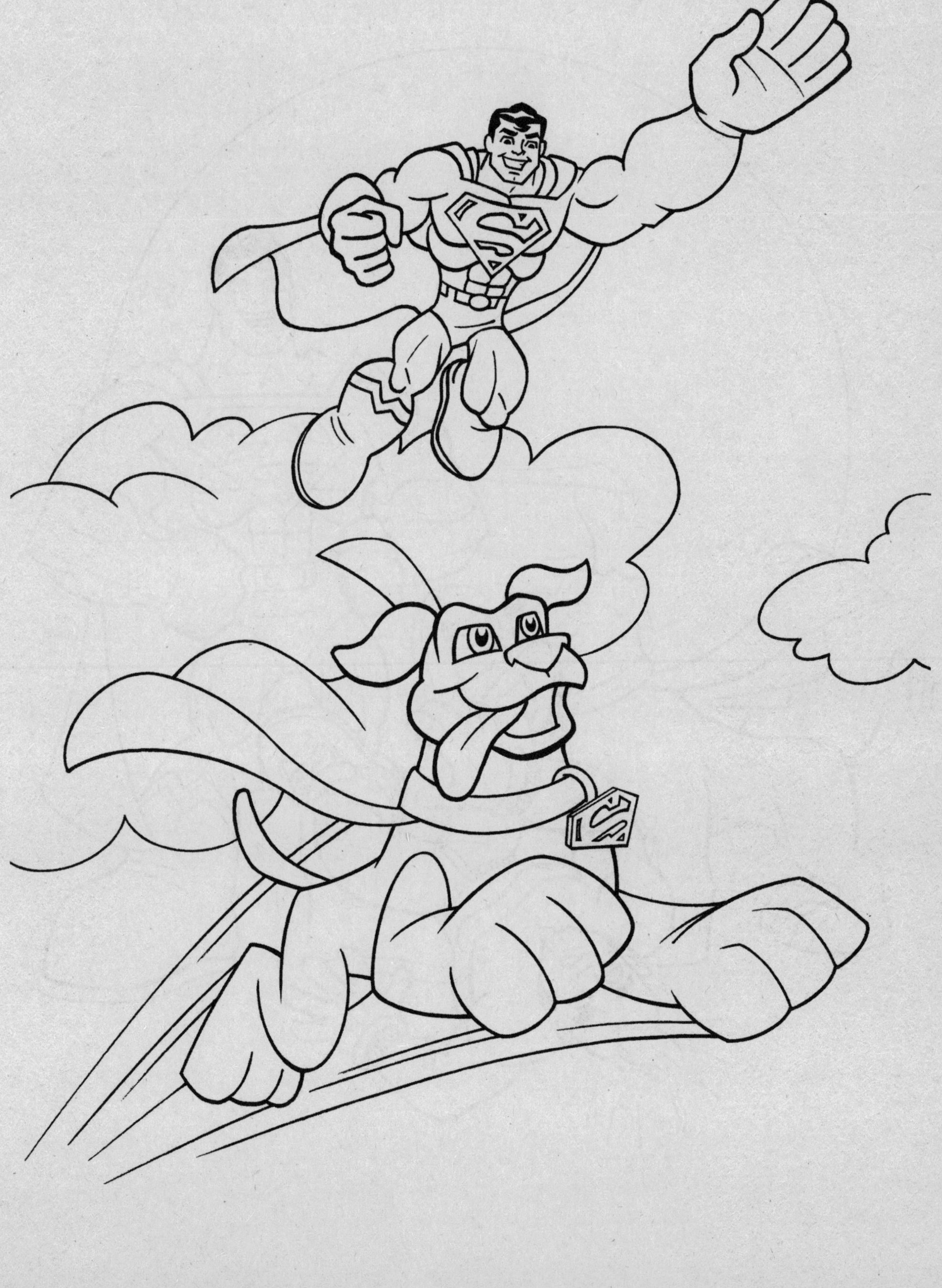

Krypto fetches the bad guys.

Krypto is lost. Help Superman find his four-legged friend.

START

FINISH

ANSWER:

The Super Friends protect the city!

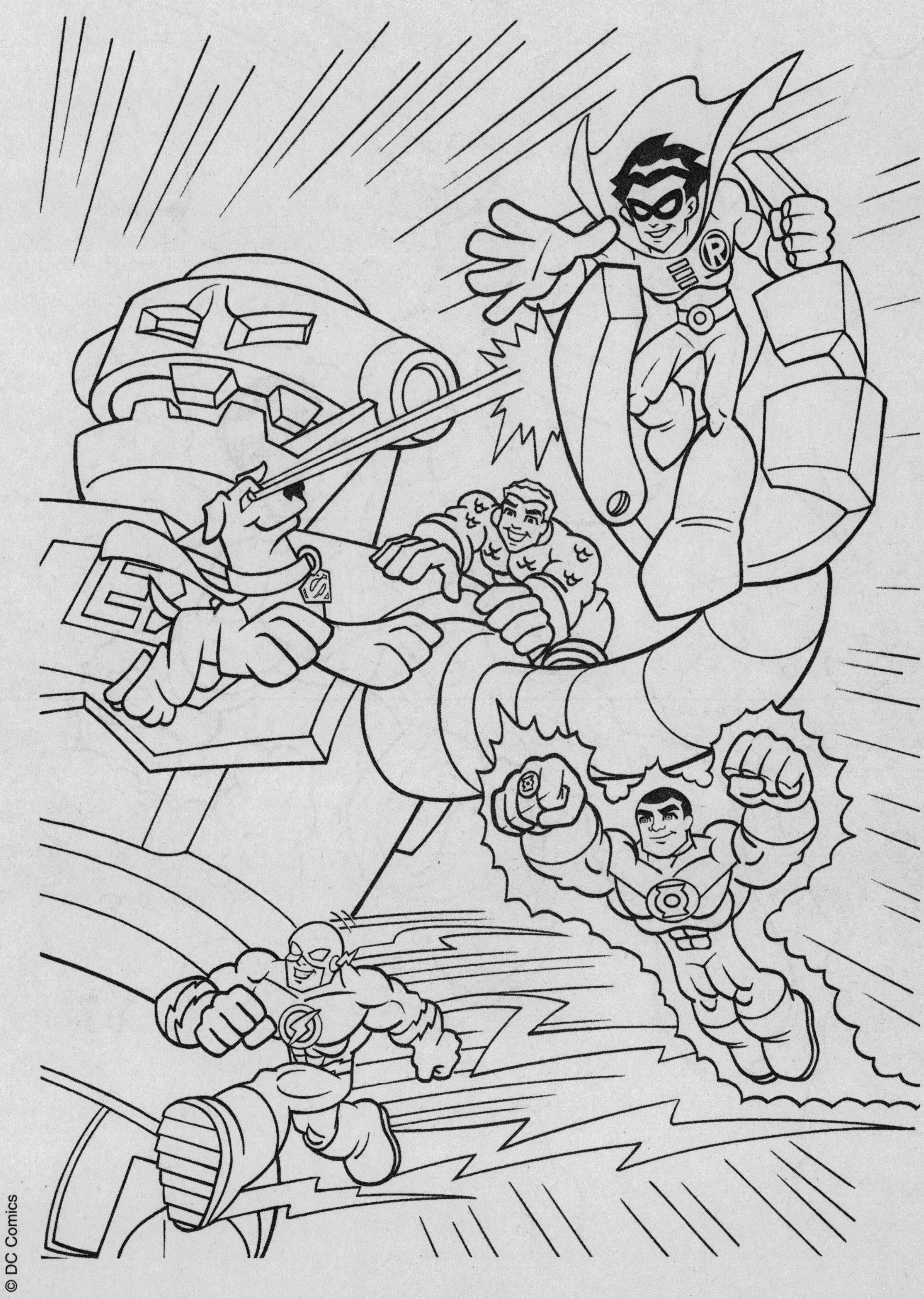

Green Lantern uses his amazing Power Ring.

Batman feels Mr. Freeze's icy touch.

Superman thaws Mr. Freeze's sinister plan!

Hawkman is also called the Winged Wonder.

Batman uses his brains as well as his brawn.

Hawkman takes flight!

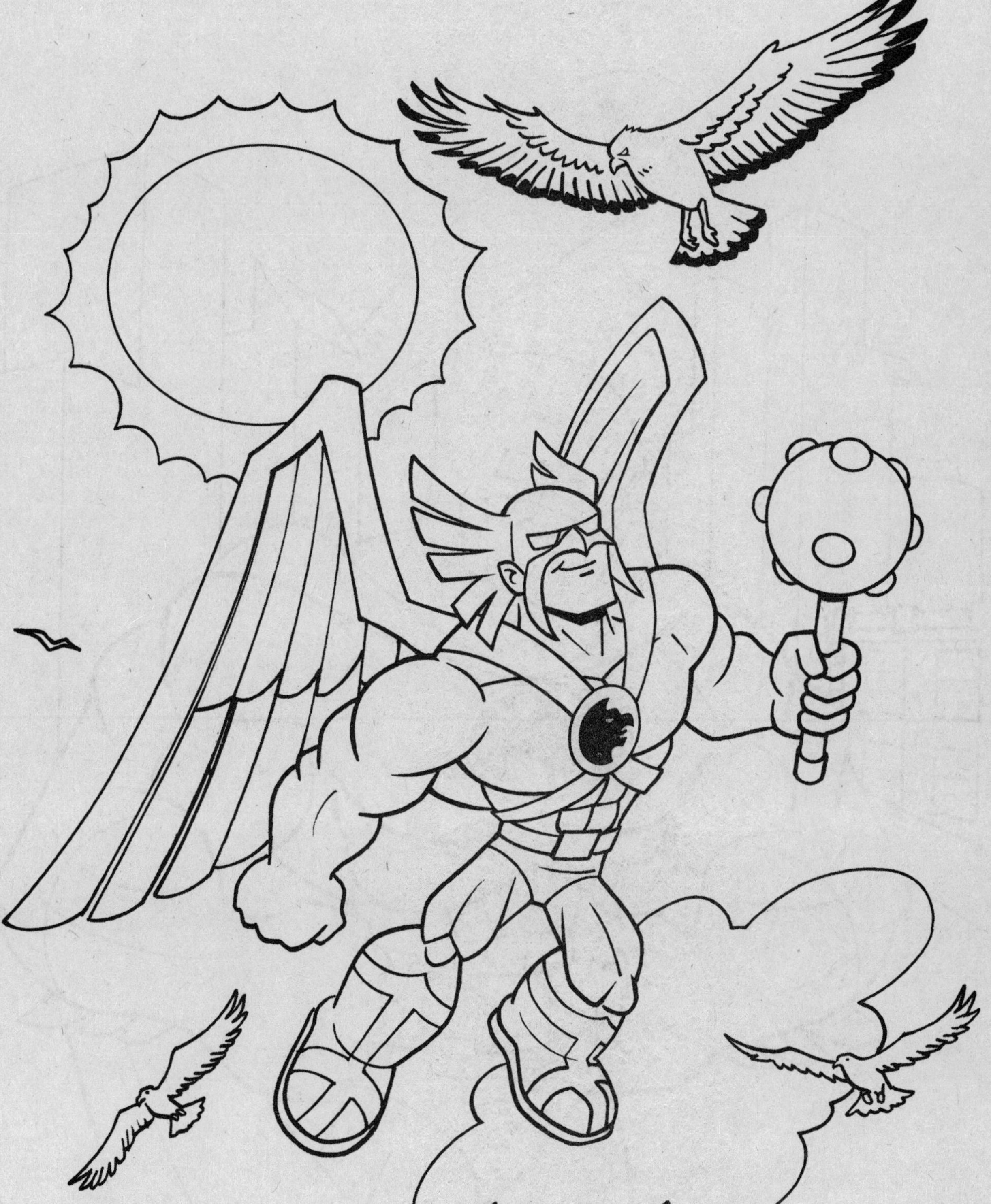

The Bat-Signal alerts Batman to trouble in Gotham City.

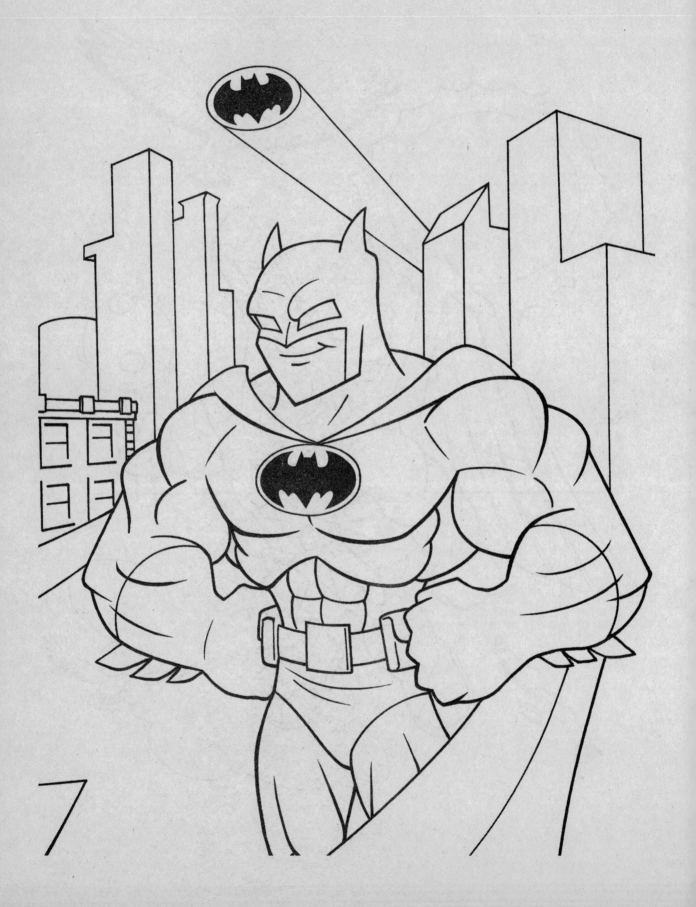

7

Cyborg is also called the Human Machine.

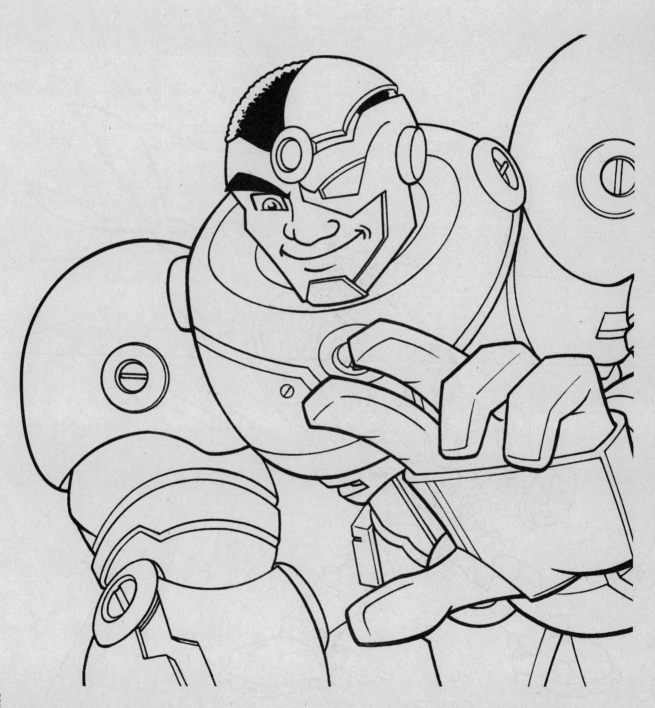

Cyborg's arm can transform into almost anything he needs.

Robin learns about crime-fighting from Batman.

Young Justice!

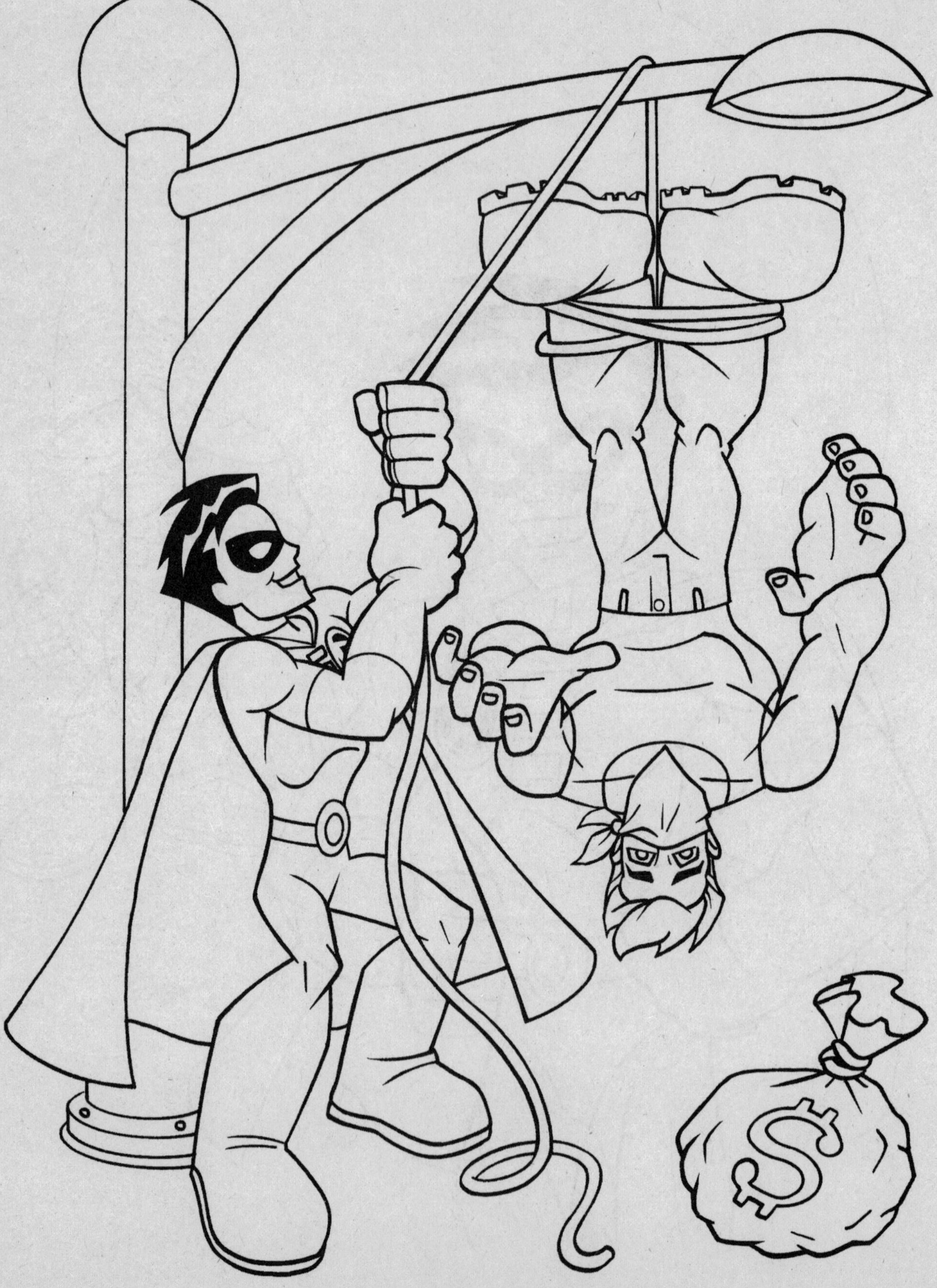

The Flash is going into overdrive!

Green Lantern is also called the Emerald Guardian.

Green Lantern can create anything he imagines with his Power Ring!

Can you find the real Superman?
(Hint: He's the one that's different.)

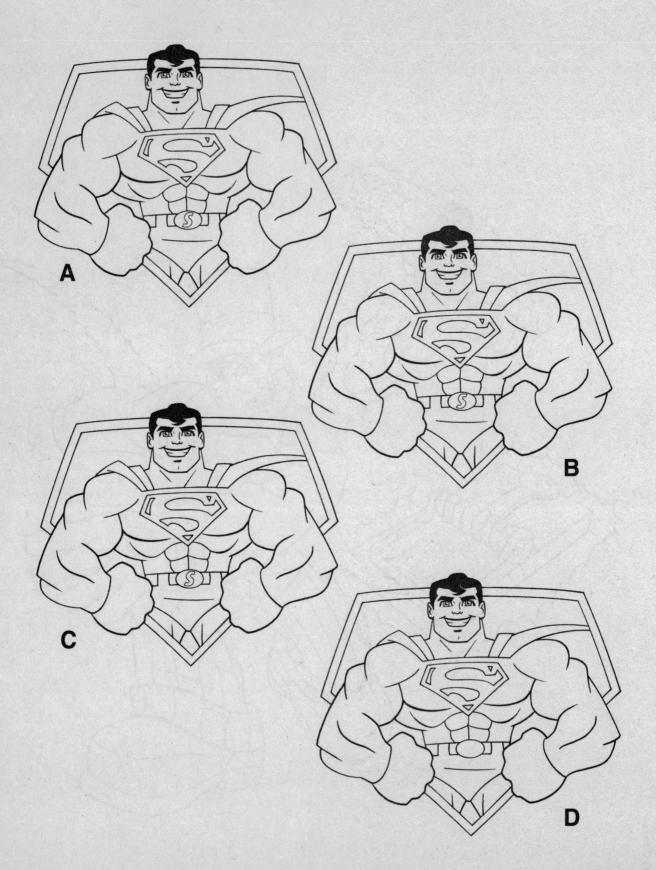

Krypto is Superman's best friend.

The Flash is faster than a bolt of lightning!

Aquaman rules the deep.

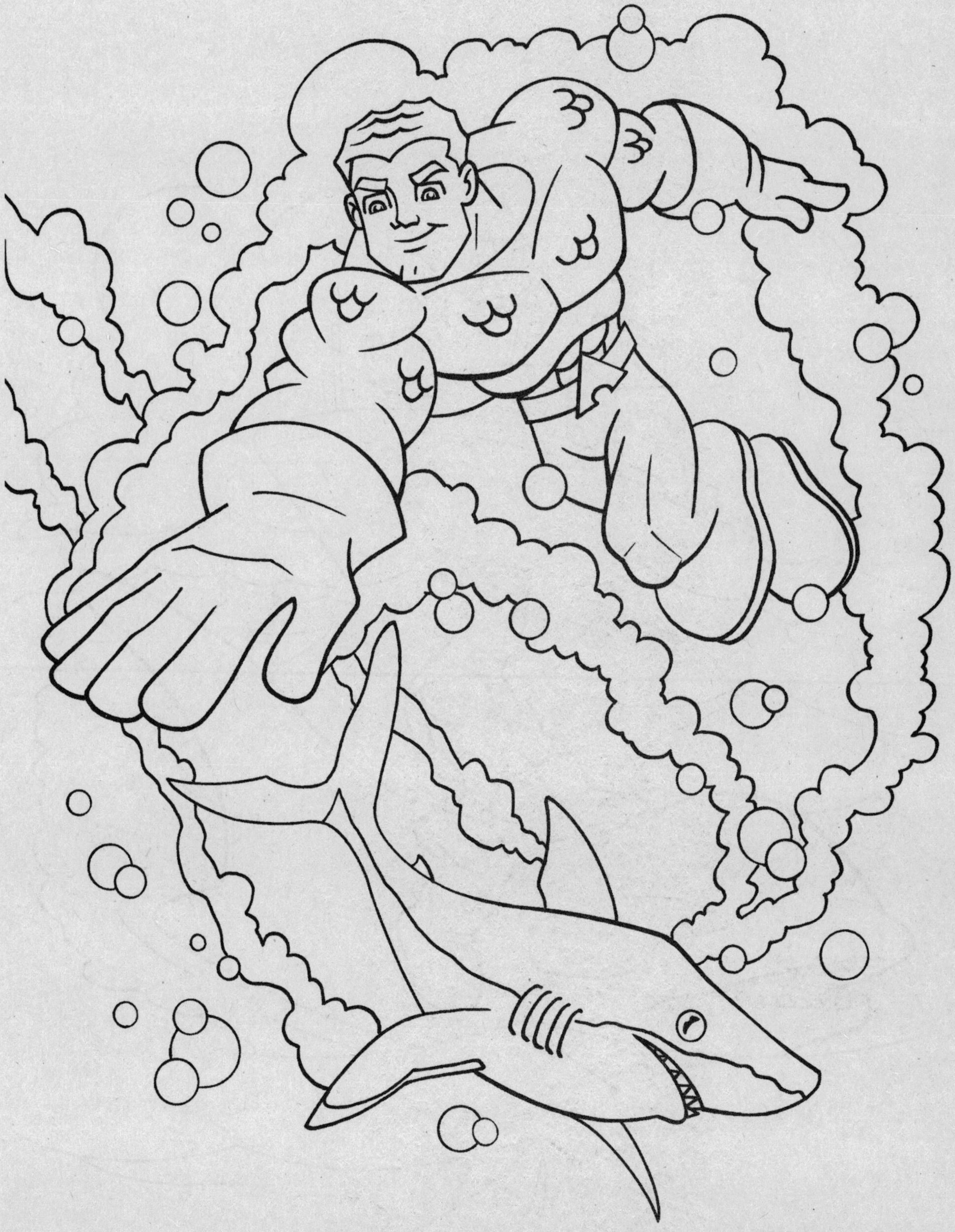

The creatures of the sea help Aquaman rescue lost ships.

Use the key to help Batman and Robin decode this message.

A	B	C	D	E	F	G	H	I	J	K	L	M	N	O	P	Q	R	S	T	U	V	W	X	Y	Z
26	25	24	23	22	21	20	19	18	17	16	15	14	13	12	11	10	9	8	7	6	5	4	3	2	1

__ __ .   __ __ __ __ __ __   __ __
14 9   21 9 22 22 1 22 18 8

__ __ __ __ __ __ __
9 12 25 25 18 13 20

__ __ __   __ __ __ __ !
7 19 22 25 26 13 16

ANSWER: Mr. Freeze is robbing the bank!

Superman is also called the Man of Steel.

Up, up, and away!

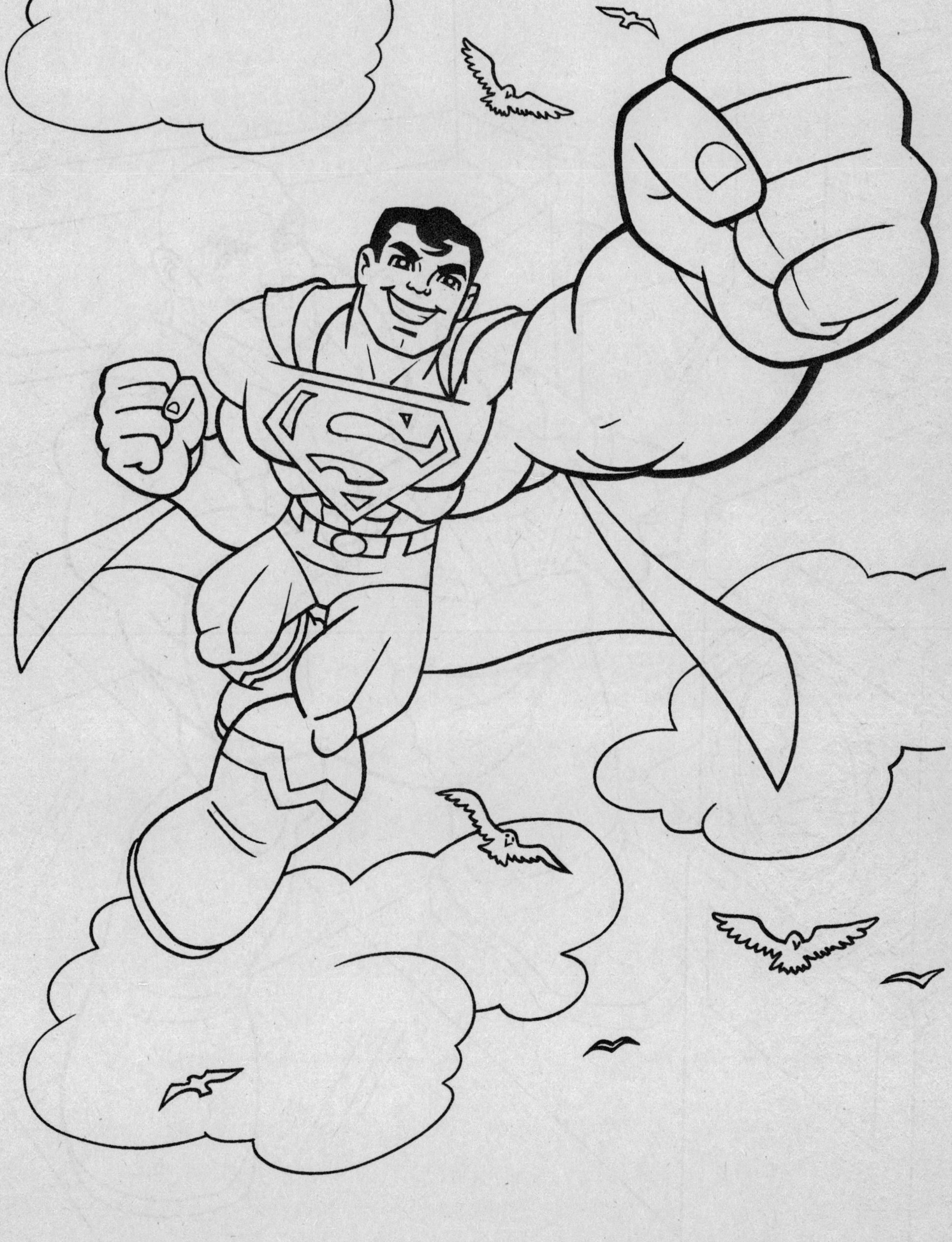

Oh, no! Lex Luthor is stealing a precious diamond!

Superman foils Lex's evil plans!

The Batmobile is a cool crime-fighting machine!

Batman watches over Gotham City.

Robin is Batman's sidekick.

The Caped Crusaders swing into action!

Robin rides the Batcycle!

Batman drops in on the Joker!

Teamwork saves the day!

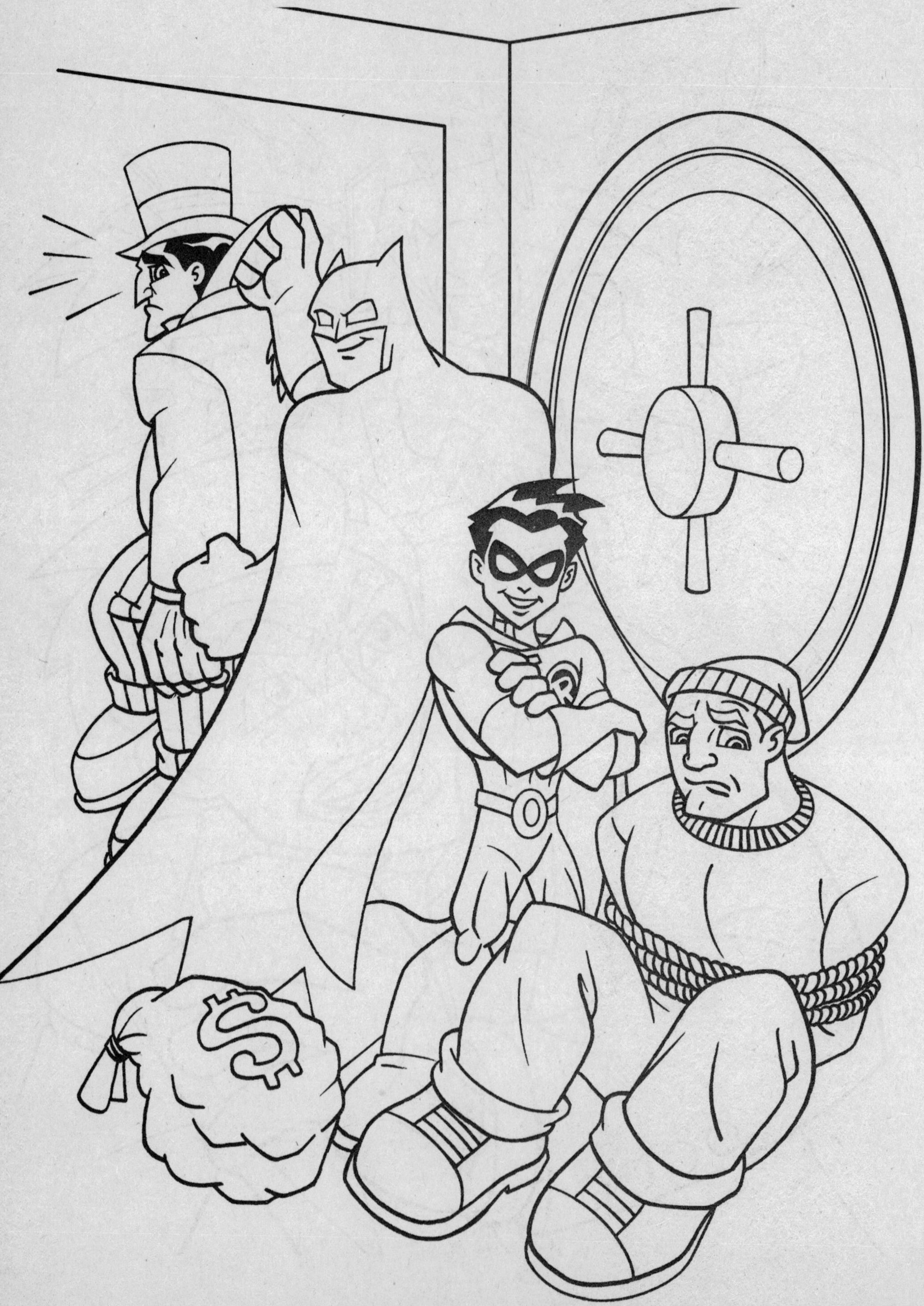

**Aquaman is the Ruler of Atlantis,
a city beneath the sea.**

Aquaman can talk to sea creatures.

Aquaman swims to the rescue!

Aquaman dives deep into the sea!

Cyborg is half man, half machine!

Cyborg battles the cold-blooded Mr. Freeze!

Whom does Batman see in the cracked fun-house mirror? Find out by using the numbers below to color the picture.

1 = white   2 = green   3 = red

4 = orange   5 = purple

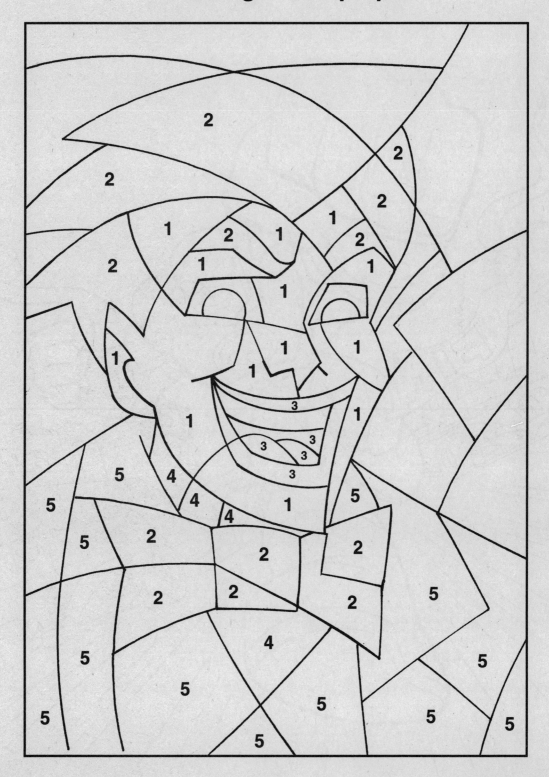

ANSWER: The Joker.

The Flash is superfast!

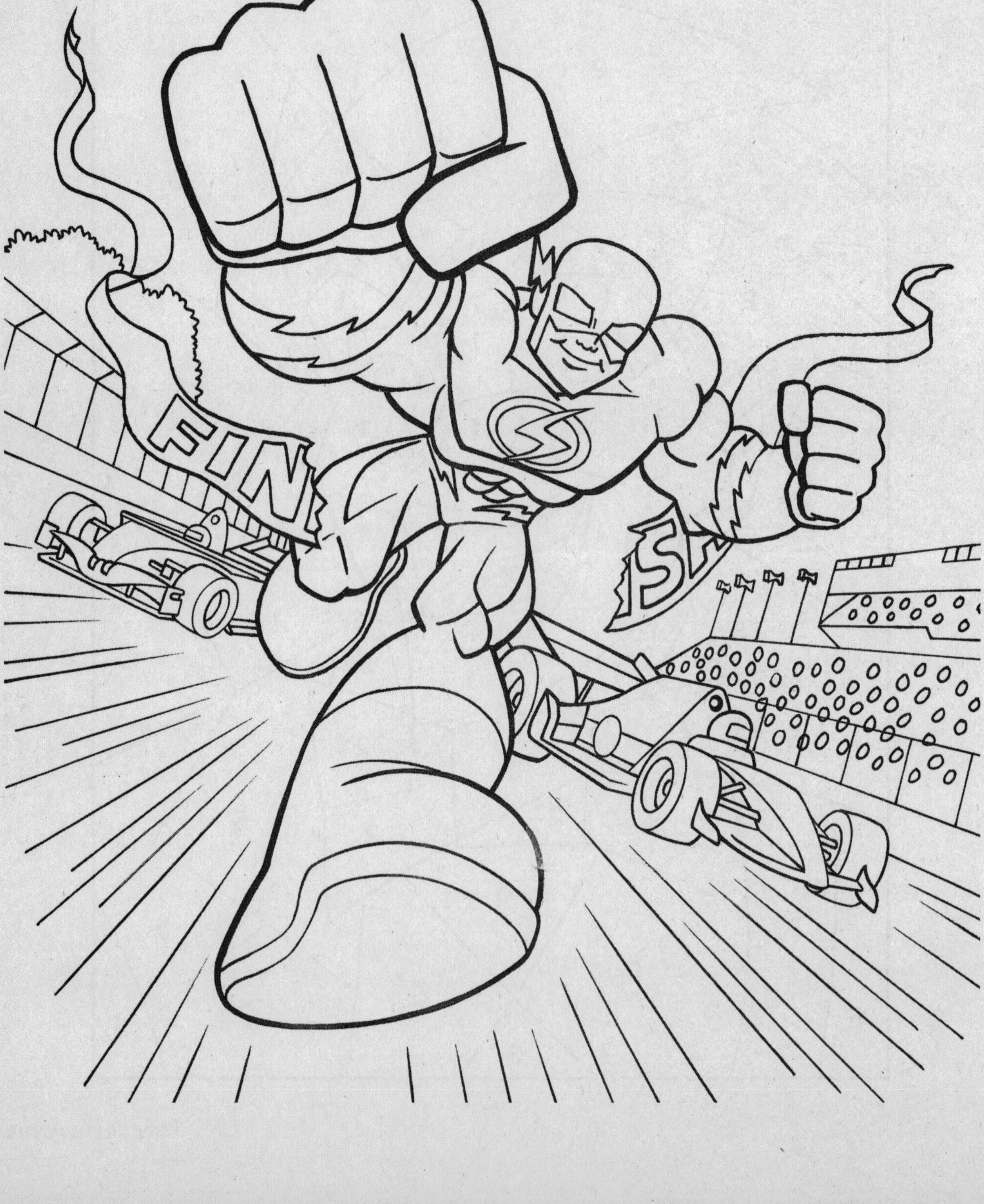
FIN
ISH

The Joker is a bad clown!

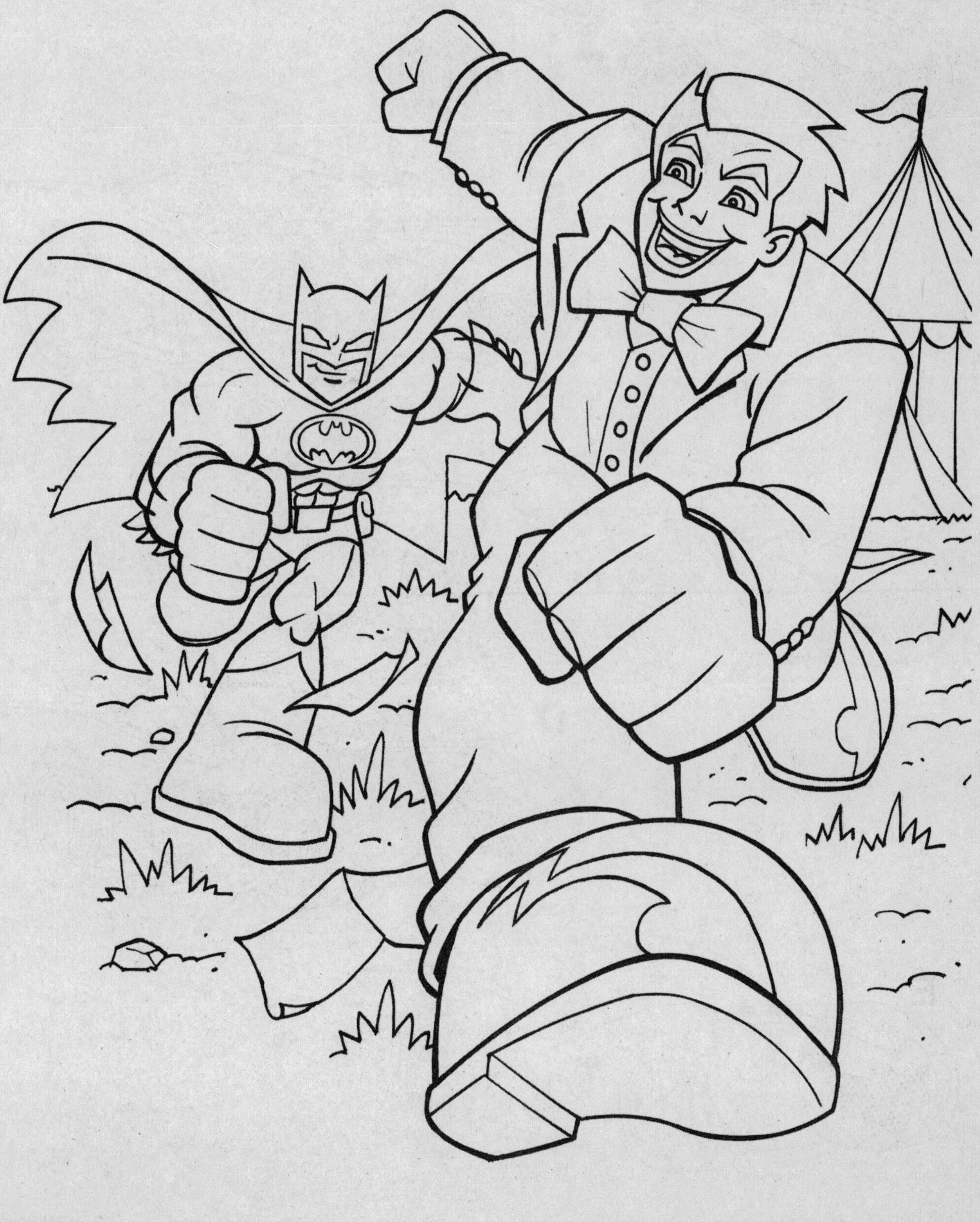

Help Batman find the real Batmobile.
Circle the one that is different.

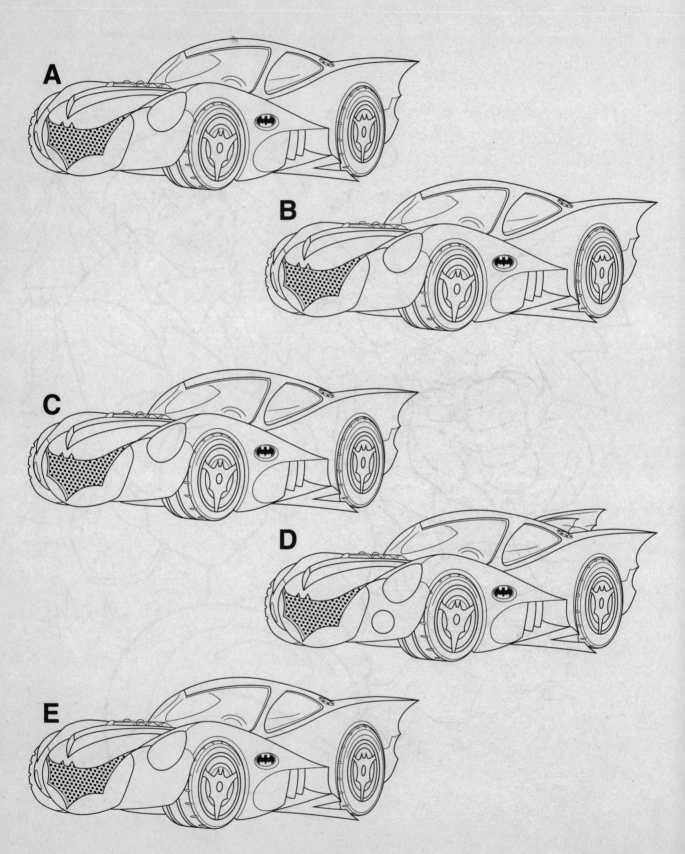

A

B

C

D

E

What is Robin's nickname? Use the code to find out.

A	B	C	D	E	F	G	H	I	J	K	L	M	N	O	P	Q	R	S	T	U	V	W	X	Y	Z
26	25	24	23	22	21	20	19	18	17	16	15	14	13	12	11	10	9	8	7	6	5	4	3	2	1

___ ___ ___   ___ ___ ___   ___ ___ ___ ___ ___ ___
7 19 22   25 12 2   4 12 13 23 22 9

ANSWER: The Boy Wonder.

Superman is flying through space. Help him escape the kryptonite meteor shower!

START

FINISH!

To finish the Green Lantern Oath, begin at the letter E and go clockwise around the circle. Write each letter on the lines below in the order they appear.

In brightest day, in blackest night, no evil shall

__ __ __ __ __ __ __ __ __ __ __ __!

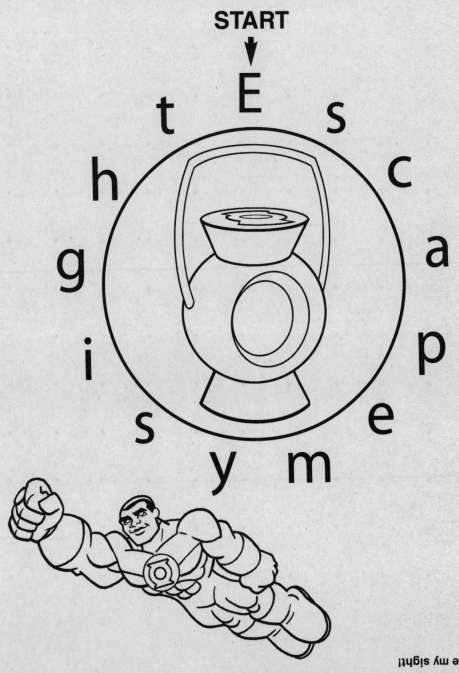

START

E t s h c g a i p s e y m

The Flash vs. the Foes!

Help the Flash round up the bad guys. Take turns with a friend connecting two dots with a straight line. When the line you draw completes a square, put your initials in the square and give yourself two points. If the square has a bad guy in it, give yourself two extra points. Whoever has more points is as fast as the Flash!

Cyborg's computer has given him a mixed-up message from Superman. Follow the line from each letter to a box. To decode the message, write the letter in the box.

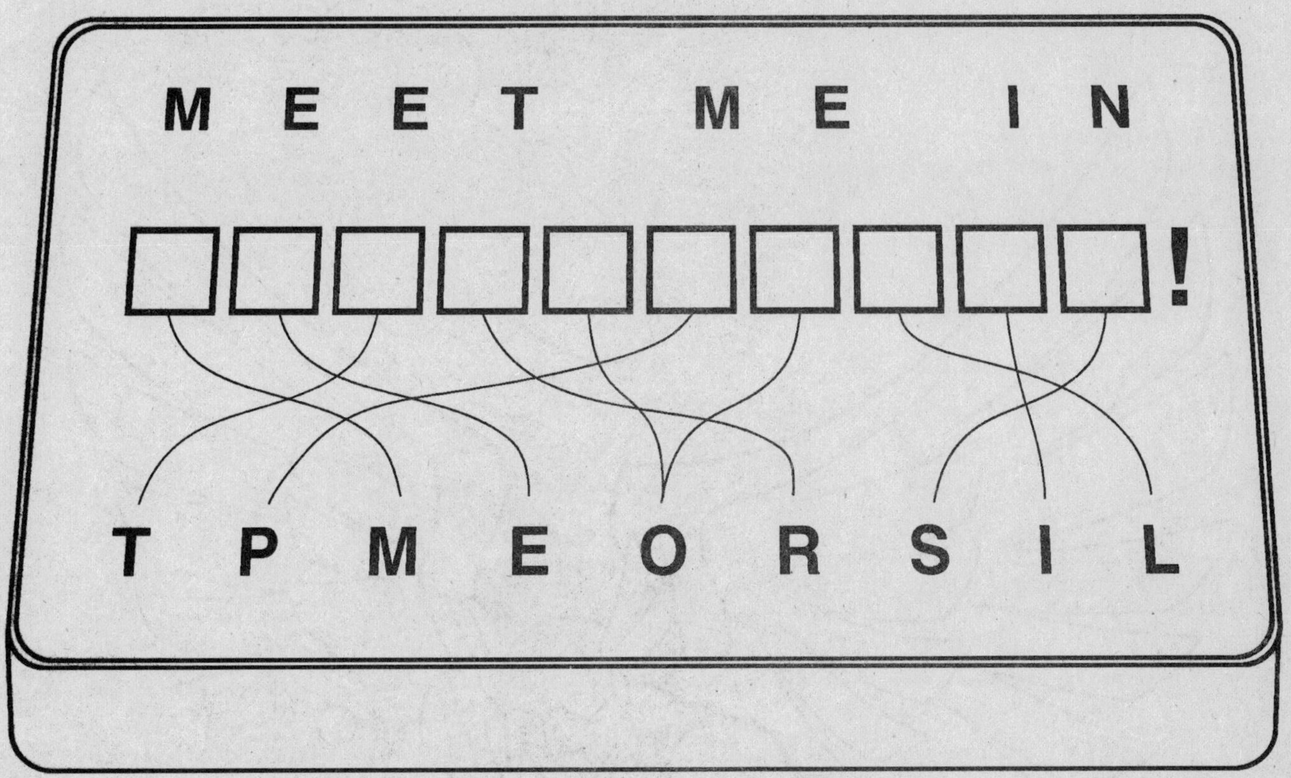
MEET ME IN
!
T P M E O R S I L

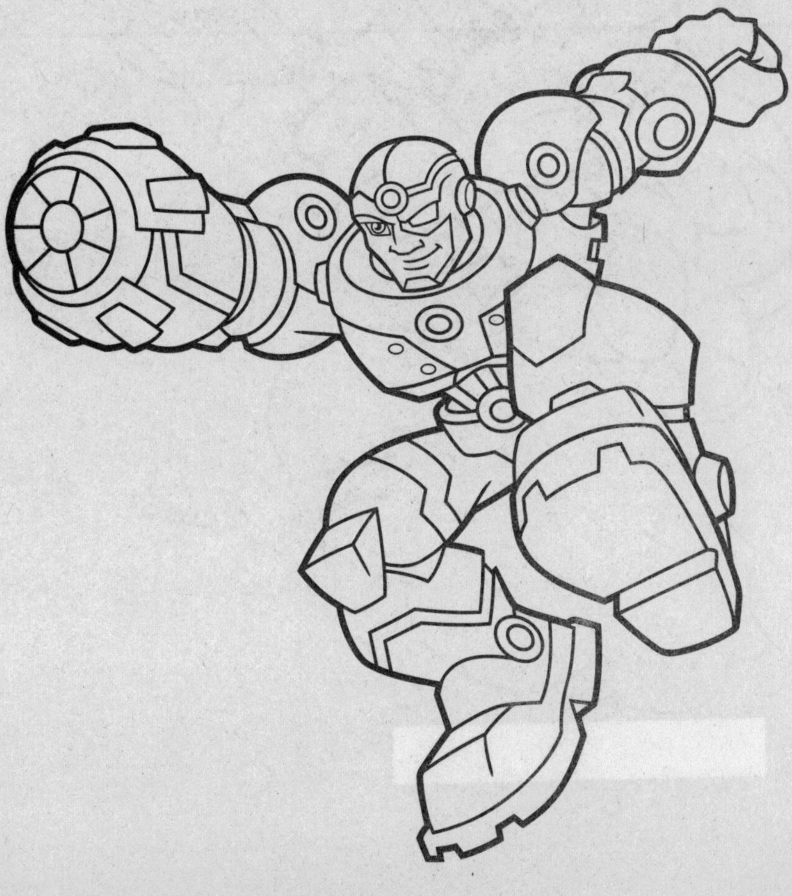

ANSWER: Meet me in Metropolis!

Hawkman flies high with his powerful wings!